Parents and Caregivers,

Stone Arch Readers are designed to provide enjoyable reading experiences, as well as opportunities to develop vocabulary, literacy skills, and comprehension. Here are a few ways to support your beginning reader:

- Talk with your child about the ideas addressed in the story.

- Discuss each illustration, mentioning the characters, where they are, and what they are doing.

- Read with expression, pointing to each word. You may want to read the whole story through and then revisit parts of the story to ensure that the meanings of words or phrases are understood.

- Talk about why the character did what he or she did and what your child would do in that situation.

- Help your child connect with characters and events in the story.

Remember, reading with your child should be fun, not forced. Each moment spent reading with your child is a priceless investment in his or her literacy life.

Gail Saunders-Smith, Ph.D.

STONE ARCH READERS

are published by Stone Arch Books, a Capstone Imprint
1710 Roe Crest Drive
North Mankato, Minnesota 56003
www.capstonepub.com

Library of Congress Cataloging-in-Publication data is available on the Library of Congress website.

ISBN 978-1-4342-4018-7 (library binding)
ISBN 978-1-4342-4239-6 (paperback)

Reading Consultants:
Gail Saunders-Smith, Ph.D.
Melinda Melton Crow, M.Ed.
Laurie K. Holland, Media Specialist

Designer: Hilary Wacholz

Printed in the United States of America, Stevens Point, Wisconsin.
062012   006788R

The Long Train Ride

written by
Melinda Melton Crow

illustrated by
Chad Thompson

STONE ARCH BOOKS
a capstone imprint

School Bus, Tractor, Fire Truck, and Train were friends.

"I need two new tires,"
said Tractor.

"I can help," said Train.

"I have to go far to get
the tires," said Train.

"Goodbye, Train!"

Train drove for two days.

He found the tire store.

The tires were big.

19

Train drove for two more days.

"Here comes Train!"
said Tractor.

"Two new tires for Tractor,"
said Train.

"Two new tires for me!"
said Tractor.

"Thank you, Train!"
said Tractor.

Look at Tractor go!

STORY WORDS

friends   help   found

tires   drove   store

Total Word Count: 82